Tales of Nokomis

Tales of Nokomis

Patronella Johnston

Illustrations by Francis Kagige

Charles J. Musson Limited

Publishers Toronto

ISBN 0-07-092873-8

The publisher gratefully acknowledges the assistance of the Canada Council.

Contents

Preface

These stories were told to me as a child, by a very old Indian lady of the Ojibwa nation who lived to her one hundred and third year.

During the winter months, I and several other children would stop at her home after school to bring in kindling and water and to pick a basket of frozen apples from the orchard, for she was too old and feeble to gather them for herself. After the chores were done, we would gather around her by the hearth. She would bake apples for us and tell us old Indian legends.

It wasn't until recently, when I started telling her stories to my foster children, that I realized how little they knew of their Indian folklore heritage. They were fascinated by the stories, so I began to put them down on paper. Otherwise they would have been gone forever.

It is to my foster children, Evelyn, Barbara, Charlene, Beth, Myles, and Derek, that I dedicate this book.

Patronella Johnston

Stories of Nanabush

Bedabin and her brother Tawa would not think of leaving their dear grandmother, Nokomis, at home, especially on the day of the school picnic.

Nokomis watched the young people's fun with much joy. There were games and races on the sandy beach, and much splashing and playing in the water afterwards. Everyone was very hungry by the time the picnic feast was ready.

After the feast, Nokomis hesitantly asked the teacher if she might tell the children some of the stories she had learned from her mother, tales of the Ojibwa people, tales of their own past.

The teacher was very pleased. She too had wanted the children to hear their own folklore. She knew that Nokomis could tell many stories, but she hadn't known quite how to ask her.

Nokomis spread her old shawl on the grass, and sat down. She looked around at the happy expectant faces, and solemnly began:

Once upon a time, long before the white man came to this beautiful country of ours, there lived a giant of a man.

He knew the best time to hunt and to fish, the best time to travel, and when to make camp and rest.

He was a special friend of the West Wind, the most powerful of all the winds, so that he could tell his people what the weather would be like for days to come.

Thus, they were never caught in a storm when they planned a hunt. They knew when to stretch their hides for tanning, and when to gather the birch bark, and many other things they needed to know for survival.

This giant of a man could change himself into any form he wished, in the twinkling of an eye.

He was also full of tricks, and could fool almost any enemy. From time to time he even tricked his own people to teach them a lesson, and he would laugh aloud at their surprise.

All his people loved him, especially the women and children. To them he could be very gentle. When the braves were away on a hunt, he would care for their families.

The people called this comical and mysterious character "Nanabush." And if you should ever cross this country, you will find that many of our Indian peoples have heard of him and tell stories about him.

Have you ever seen a lizard? It's a little brown creature that can travel quickly on land or in water. Nanabush was the one who made the lizards look as they do.

Once upon a time there used to be all kinds of evil spirits roaming around. Some caused the pumpkin and squash to mould when they were hung to dry. Others made the sap go sour at maple sugar harvest.

Some caused little children to venture into deep water when they were swimming, and made them drown.

These spirits could take any form they wished, and they caused much trouble.

One day Nanabush was lying half asleep and half awake behind a big rock. He heard the women busily stretching hides for tanning. Then he heard some grumbling, so he decided to peek around the rock to watch.

There were quite a number of women working together stretching the hides. But Nanabush saw something they were not aware of. As soon as they would finish a hide, one of the young

Nanabush changes the evil spirits into lizards.

maidens would run her fingers around the outside of the hide, and immediately the thongs that held it to the frame would break.

Nanabush knew that this was the work of the evil spirits, who this time had hidden themselves in the form of a young maiden.

He quietly approached the young girl. As he drew near, the spirits saw him and started to withdraw. But wise old Nanabush knew what to do.

"I work for good, and you work for evil," he said. "I'll tell you what we will do. Race me to the edge of the lake. If you catch me before I reach the shore, then the evil spirits will be master."

The evil spirits were full of joy. They felt sure that because they were so powerful, and because there were so many of them, they would be sure to catch Nanabush.

Off started Nanabush, with the evil spirits right behind. Faster and faster he went, the evil spirits gaining all the time.

The women stood frozen with fear that the evil spirits would catch Nanabush. All the braves were away, so they could not help if the giant fell to the evil forces.

Nanabush went straight on towards the lake, gaining speed as he went. The spirits were so intent upon following him that they did not notice they were nearly at the water's edge.

As Nanabush reached the lake, he changed into a swan, and swam gracefully out on the water.

But the evil spirits were going so fast they could not stop. They went flying into the water, hitting their heads on the sharp rocks near the shore. Chump, chump, chump, they went, every last one of them.

Nanabush did not let them die, but allowed them to sink down to the bottom of the lake. He decided that from that time on they would take the form of lizards, and would live in the water. They would be allowed to come on land only at night, when everyone was fast asleep.

Nanabush and the Skunk

One day Nanabush was returning from a visit to friends in a faraway part of the forest. He had been travelling for many days and was very tired and hungry. He decided that if he was to have the strength to return to his people, he would have to kill and eat the very next animal he saw.

But the wise old owl must have sent out a warning with the swift weasel and the night hawks: "Take cover, for Nanabush is on his way, and he is very hungry." On and on he went for miles without seeing any living creature.

Poor Nanabush was so tired and weak that he could hardly drag one big foot after the other. He just had to have some food.

Finally he appealed to his good friend, the West Wind.

"West Wind, West Wind," he called. "Please help me, or I will be sure to perish here."

West Wind was playing with an old Elm, watching her sway in his gentle breeze, when he heard Nanabush call. With a big swoop he dashed through the forest, pushing everything out of his way as he sped to reach his friend.

The animals in the forest huddled very close in their beds when they saw the trees swaying and heard the wind roar. They were sure that a big storm had arisen.

When West Wind reached Nanabush he asked, "What can I do for you, my friend?"

The skunk's descendants still carry the scent given them by the West Wind.

"Give me food, food," whispered poor Nanabush, so weak he could just barely be heard.

"This I can't do," said the West Wind. "Even with all my power, I am not allowed to take the life of any bird or animal. But I will tell you what I will do. I will make a fast trip through the forest, and if I see an animal I will give it a scent that you can follow to reach the creature."

It wasn't long before a powerful scent reached Nanabush. He followed it until he came to a small black animal with a white stripe down its back. He knew at first glance that it was the skunk.

The poor skunk was mortified. In tears he said, "Nanabush, I don't know what has happened to me. I never smelled like this before. Now none of my friends will want to come near me."

Nanabush laughed, and explained that his friend the West Wind had given the little skunk the smell so that Nanabush could survive. He also explained that he would have to eat the skunk to gain strength to finish his journey to his people.

Then he added, "As a reward for saving my life, all your descendants will have this scent. None of your enemies will bother you, and you will live in peace for all the days to come."

From that day onwards, the skunk has carried the scent bestowed upon him by the friend of Nanabush.

The Red and White Trillium

Nokomis and her grandchildren spent many long hours in the woods and beside the stream near the encampment of their people. One day Bedabin and Tawa were walking with Nokomis when they came upon a little stream shining in the sun.

"Oh, Nokomis, Tawa, look!" Bedabin exclaimed. Usually she spoke softly, as she had been taught by her parents and her grandmother. But this time she could hardly contain herself, and she clasped her hands with joy. "It is so beautiful!"

"Just like a ribbon of gold, not a stream at all," Nokomis added softly.

"It seems," mused Bedabin, "that when the Great Manitou made something, he never intended for it to be only useful. He always made it beautiful too."

"That's right," agreed Nokomis. "Do you know," she added, "that when in the beginning he created the earth and all its creatures, everything was white? It was only after the creation that he painted the earth the beautiful colours it is today."

"Do tell us more," asked the children.

"Well," said Nokomis, "first he painted the animals. He used mostly browns and greys."

"Like the rabbit and the wolf," said Tawa.

"But he often added a little red or black to give the animals lovely soft variations in colour."

"Like the fox and the fawn," said Bedabin.

"And all these animals were then not only useful, but they were beautiful too," Nokomis continued. "But sometimes in winter, when the leaves had fallen from the trees and it is difficult to hide in safety, he allows some of the animals to return to their original white. That way they will not be as readily seen by their enemies."

"Like the rabbit and ermine," said Tawa. "They can hide very easily in the white snow."

"And the trees," Nokomis went on, "were all white in the beginning, too. But the Great Manitou gave to them and the grass the colour of green. Sometimes he added a little yellow or orange, so that there were many different shades of green, but all blended well together. And he found the trees useful, and very soothing and peaceful to look upon."

"Were the flowers white in the beginning, too?" asked Bedabin.

"Yes, indeed," said Nokomis.

"Oh, I am glad he decided to change that," said Bedabin.

"For the flowers he used every possible colour," Nokomis explained. "Pink Arbutus and pink Lady's Slipper . . . ."

"And deep purple Violets and blue-purple Gentians," added Bedabin.

"And yellow Violets too," said Tawa, not to be outdone. "And yellow Lilies."

"Yes, the Great Manitou really showed his love of colour when he made the flowers," said Nokomis. "But he never quite finished painting them."

"Why not?" asked Tawa.

"Well, he painted the flowers last of all," said Nokomis, "And there were lots and lots of them. Think of all the forests of the world, all full of flowers."

"And all the plains and the mountains and deserts," added Bedabin.

"The Great Manitou was growing very tired," continued Nokomis.

"His hand must have been very heavy," said Tawa. "It would have taken many moons to do all that painting."

"And he was tired of thinking, too," added Nokomis. "Imagine thinking of different colours for all of those flowers. All that remained of the paint was a small portion in the red pot. He had saved this for the Trillium. But the Great Manitou had coloured only a few of them when he found the red paint all gone. That is why, if you take a walk in the woods today, you will find a few red Trilliums, but most of them are still pure, beautiful white, just as they were when the Creator ran out of red paint."

The Indian Paint Brush

Nokomis taught Bedabin and Tawa all she knew of the creatures of nature. It was their schoolroom. When he grew up, Tawa would have to know of all the animals of the woods and of all their habits, for he would use this knowledge when he went hunting with the other men. On this learning would depend the survival of his future family.

But it was also a joy to learn of the ways of other living creatures, like oneself, who each had a soul and a power.

Nokomis taught the children to walk with caution, keeping as silent as possible. Then they would not frighten the animals away, and they could observe them.

Also, if they walked softly, they could hear the slightest motion or sound. They could hear a muskrat or beaver long before they could spot it in the river.

Many times they had lain motionless along the riverbank, while a mother beaver brought her young for a swim, and gave them their first lesson in dam building.

Tawa and Bedabin had stood perfectly still in the middle of a clump of cedars while a mother partridge strutted by, followed by as many as eighteen bundles of fuzz. At the slightest sound, the baby partridges would disappear under leaves or rotted logs or anything which would hide them. Meanwhile the mother bird flopped and fluttered around to draw attention to herself, and away from her children.

One day, when returning from a walk in the woods with her grandmother and her brother, Bedabin stopped to pick a bouquet of Indian Paint Brush. She loved the long soft tassels of red, and knew that her mother would, too.

Nokomis had taught the children to be careful when they picked flowers – not to take any of the young buds, and not to pick too many. But it was fine to pick flowers as a gift, or to look at back in the encampment.

Bedabin held up her bouquet for her brother and grandmother to see.

"How lovely," exclaimed Nokomis. "And it is just the right time to pick them too – at the end of the day."

"Why is that?" asked Tawa with interest.

"Well," explained Nokomis, "just as evening comes at the end of the day, so the Indian Paint Brush was the last flower which the Great Manitou created."

"I remember," said Tawa, "that you told us that everything was white to begin with."

"And that the Great Manitou painted all creatures of the earth beautiful colours," added Bedabin.

"Yes," said Nokomis. "That's the way the story goes. And when he had finished painting the last trillium red . . . ."

"But there wasn't enough paint to colour them all," interrupted Tawa.

"That's so," agreed Nokomis, smiling. "But when he had painted the last one that he possibly could, then he flung away his paint brush, all covered still with red paint. And where it landed, grew the beautiful tassels of the Indian Paint Brush."

The Jewel Weed

One day Nokomis was busy washing roots for winter needs. She scrubbed hard at the roots to remove all the dirt from them, and rinsed them well in the clear water of the stream. Then she spread them all on the ground to dry, separating them according to the various uses to which they would be put. The clean, dry roots would later be ground into powder and mixed with other herbs to make various medicines.

All along, Nokomis had heard her two grandchildren laughing merrily in a damp swampy spot not far from where she was working. After a short rest, she decided to go and see what they were finding so hilarious.

They were in the midst of a large patch of Jewel Weed, having a contest to see who could get a green seed-pod to explode into the largest circle, and laughing with glee at each explosion.

Nokomis was disturbed. It was wrong to harm any plant, and especially this one. Her own mother had told her many times that she must never disturb the Touch-Me-Not, as she called it.

"Bedabin, Tawa, do stop!" she cried.

"It's fun," insisted Tawa. "Just look at this large pod. Watch and see how far it will scatter its seeds."

He pinched the pod between thumb and finger, and it exploded into many tiny particles.

"Don't you know," scolded Nokomis," that when you explode

ago . . . ."

"That our people gather the wild rice in September," interrupted Tawa.

"Right," continued Nokomis. "As they gather the rice in the marshes, they sometimes touch certain plants which give them very bad rashes. The Jewel Weed is used to cure these rashes."

"Oh," said Tawa solemnly.

"If you continue to explode these pods before they have dropped their precious seeds to the ground," added Nokomis, "there won't be as many next year to cure the rashes of our people."

"We are really sorry, Nokomis," said Bedabin seriously. "We didn't know."

"I'll never explode another," promised Tawa.

Winter Stories Only

Autumn had come to the forest, and it was beautiful beyond description. The wonderful maple tree was like fire with red hot coals gleaming in the sun, all shades of gold, brown, yellow, and red. The slender leaves of the sumac trees were deep scarlet.

Nokomis, Bedabin, and Tawa were walking down the path to the lake, past all their favourite places. The brilliant colours made the familiar path look much more regal and splendid.

It should have been beautiful enough to make everyone happy, but Bedabin looked pensive and sad.

"What is the matter, little grand-daughter?" asked Nokomis. "Enjoy the autumn sun, for soon the weather will be cold. I will no longer be able to walk with you then, little one."

"That is why I am sad," said Bedabin. "When you can no longer come with us, the fun will be gone from our walks."

Nokomis smiled, for she knew that as soon as the snow came, Badabin and Tawa would be the first outside. They would enjoy their walks just as much as before.

"It will be fun to walk in the snow. Just you wait and see," she told them both. "And I will still be able to tell you stories in the winter. After all, winter is the real time to tell stories."

"But you've told us stories all summer long," said Bedabin.

"I really should not have done so," explained Nokomis. "I have broken a very ancient Indian custom by telling stories in the summertime."

"What a silly custom," said Tawa quickly. "Stories are good all year 'round."

"It was a wise custom," Nokomis said seriously. "Our fathers saw that with all the work to be done in the summer, there was very little time for stories. There would be plenty of time during the winter months.

"In the early spring the whole band gathered sap from the maple trees. The sap was put in birch-bark vessels, then hot stones would be dropped into it to make it boil until it was thick. As it cooled, it hardened and could be stored for food the following winter.

"All summer long the women picked berries and dried them, for use during the long winter.

"The men were hard at work, too. In the early spring and summer they would kill beaver and other small game, as well as fish such as pickerel and pike. Later on they would spear larger fish, such as trout, whitefish, and sturgeon.

"They would bring their catch home to the women. Some of it would be eaten then; the rest would be cleaned and laid to dry on racks in the sun. This dried fish and game would provide food for the winter, when the snow lay on the ground and there were sometimes not many animals to be found.

"In early September our men and women would gather and dry the wild rice and pack it into bags, ready for winter meals.

"The women also had to prepare blankets and clothes for their families from the skins of the animals their men had killed. They would scrape the skins clean with stone or bone scrapers. They would dry and stretch the skins on racks and knead them to make them soft. It was a hard task that took many days.

"And that wasn't the end of their work, for once the skins were prepared, the women had to cut them with stone knives to make clothes. For needles, the women used bones, and for thread, sinew.

They had to protect their fingers with thimbles made of bone or skin, because it was hard work to pull and push the sinew through the skins.

"The women worked very hard, even harder than the men. But the men worked hard, too. Now you can see why there was little time for stories in the summer. It was wise of the chiefs to enforce this rule.

"There would be time enough for stories in the winter, when the snow lay on the ground too deep and cold for the hunters to venture outdoors. Then telling stories would help to pass the time they spent indoors."

The Burdock

As soon as the children arrived home from school, Nokomis sent them out to pick Burdock leaves.

This puzzled Bedabin, for it was already October, and the air was quite cool. It was only in the spring that Nokomis made a bitter tea from the burdock leaves. Without fail, as soon as the leaves were large enough to pick, Nokomis would send the children out to gather them.

Bedabin never minded picking them at that time of year, for the growth in the fields was just beginning, and it was easy to walk across the meadows then. In the spring too, there were no small black Burdock seeds, the kind that always stuck to you.

Bedabin rubbed her fingers together to keep them warm. She had already picked about twenty of the big leaves. They were quite pretty to look at – very large, and shaped like hearts. Surely, with the ones that Tawa had gathered, there would be enough for Nokomis. She would pick just one more.

Just as she bent over to pluck the leaf, Tawa slapped a handful of the sticky burrs in her long black hair.

Oh, what a mean trick. How she hated those burrs. Combing her hair tonight would hurt so much.

"Please don't," pleaded Bedabin. "How will I ever get them out?"

She remembered how hard it was to pick them off the dogs,

after they had been running through the fields. One by one – it took such a long time to remove them all.

"Cut your hair short like mine," laughed Tawa.

"You are just like all boys," grumbled Bedabin, "always teasing someone smaller than yourself."

Nokomis smiled when she saw the burrs in Bedabin's hair.

"Thank you for the leaves, little one," she said. "I see they cost you some effort."

Nokomis sat down on the animal skins which were spread on the ground of the dwelling, and began to sort the leaves. The largest and smoothest and most tender of them she wrapped around her leg.

"Why are you doing that?" asked Bedabin, quite puzzled.

"Because I am old," answered Nokomis. "My legs ache with the cramp, and I know that the Burdock leaves will relieve, at least for a short time, some of the discomfort."

"You know a great deal, grandmother," said Tawa with admiration. "I will always come to you when I am sick."

"Your mother knows, too," added Nokomis. "Most of the women of our people know how to treat sickness and pain. But the older ones are most wise. They have had more time to learn."

"I know," interrupted Bedabin, "all about the balsam gum."

"Awful sticky stuff from an old fir tree," said Tawa, "but if you fall and cut yourself, it will heal the wound."

"That's very true," agreed Nokomis. "The Great Manitou has looked after his children well. He has provided healing powers all around them. And he has made wise men who know how to use these powers."

"The *mede*?" asked Bedabin.

"One of the members belongs to our village," added Tawa.

"Yes, we are fortunate," said Nokomis. "The Grand Medicine Society of the Ojibwa is composed of many honoured men and women. Our member has reached the third of the four grades. He

The healing power of the Burdock.

has much healing power."

"I am glad the Great Manitou looks after us so well," said Bedabin.

"Even when you get burrs in your hair?" asked Nokomis with a smile.

"You will spend many hours taking those seeds from your hair," continued Nokomis. "But remember that at the same time you will be dropping the seed in many places. The Good Spirit made the Burdock this way so that living creatures would carry the seed far and wide, and many people could share in its great healing power."

The First Corn

Nokomis took down the braid of corn cobs from the storehouse wall, and scraped the corn from the cobs, very thoroughly. She took off every kernel. As she was working, the spoke to her grandchildren.

"We are fortunate to have golden corn to eat. Not all of our people do. The Ojibwa who live further north do not grow it. But we grow a little. The men prepare the fields, and the women plant and harvest it."

"My mother works in the fields, too," Tawa added.

After Nokomis had removed all the corn, she placed the bare cobs and husks in an old box in the storehouse.

"Everything must be saved that can be used," she said. "From the husks we will weave mats for the floors of our houses."

"And we lay our skins on the husks and sleep on them," Tawa added.

The children followed Nokomis into the house. They watched as she sifted some hardwood ashes. They were grey, and made her fingers all dirty. She was about to prepare their favourite food – Indian corn.

Soon the ashes were ready. Nokomis poured water into an iron kettle until it was half full. Then she added the sifted ashes.

"How fortunate we are to have a kettle," Nokomis said. "In the olden days, food took a long time to cook. First, the women had

As the spirit warrior falls, he breaks into many pieces.

to heat stones in the fire. Then they would place the very hot stones in birch-bark containers filled with water. The water would become hot, and the food would cook."

"Now, Bedabin, bring the corn and watch carefully, for some day you will be doing the same thing for your own children."

After Bedabin had brought the corn, Nokomis placed the heavy pot over the fire. After a long time, little bubbles began to appear on the surface. Then the water started to jump about. It was time to put in the corn.

Nokomis poured in the kernels, very carefully, so as not to splash hot water on the children. With a long wooden paddle, she began to stir the corn.

Once in a while she would remove a few grains from the pot, pour cold water on them, and run the kernels between her fingers to see if they were cooked.

"Nokomis, where did corn come from?" Tawa asked.

"It is a very lovely story," said Nokomis. "Let's wait until the corn is finished. Then I will tell you the story of the first corn."

Nokomis carefully removed the kettle from the fire. She lifted out the corn, and washed it free of every trace of ashes. Then she placed it in a clean kettle, with fresh water, and brought it again to a boil.

Then she put it again in fresh water, and heated it until there were small bubbles on the surface.

By this time, Tawa and Bedabin could hardly sit still. But like good Indian children, they did as they were told.

"Just a minute more," said Nokomis. "I'm almost ready."

She lifted the corn from the water, washed it for a last time, and put it in a cool place to store for use the next day.

"Now for our story," said Tawa.

"Many moons ago," Nokomis began, "long before the white man ever came to our land, a young brave brought corn to our people. . . "

Now as you know, when Indian boys and girls become young men and women, they have to go off, all by themselves, into a small wigwam. There they fast several days, with nothing to eat and only a little water to drink.

If the young person does just what he should do, the good spirit will come to him in a vision and tell him just what he must do with his life, and how he can best help his people.

It is very difficult. But it is part of growing up.

A long time ago, a young brave, a little older than Tawa, had reached the right age for the vision to occur. He went off all by himself to a wigwam and ate nothing at all for several days.

The people were sure that the good spirit would show a great vision to this boy, for he was both strong and kind. He would be sure to bring a mighty gift to his people.

A few days later, the boy came out of the wigwam. He was very weak from hunger, and could hardly stand.

Everyone waited in silence for him to speak.

"I have indeed seen a vision," he assured them. "But I do not know what it means."

"Describe the vision to me," the chief, a very wise man, said quietly.

"A great warrior came to me, and engaged me in a duel," said the young boy. "His body was strong and brown from the sun. We wrestled for a long time. There were times when I was sure he would defeat me, but I fought back with all my strength.

"At long last, I vanquished my foe. When I did, he fell apart into many little pieces."

The wise chief then said, "Go again into the wigwam. Do not eat anything, and the vision will come again. I believe your mission has not yet been completed."

The young brave did as the chief commanded.

The great warrior came to him again in a vision. This time he came in peace.

"I am the corn," he said softly. "Because you have vanquished me, I now give myself to you. Your people must go their way for the summer, but when the leaves fall, they must return to this place. You will then find me growing in great numbers. Gather me carefully, for I will be one of your mainstays for life."

In the morning, the young brave went to the chief, and told the older man what he had heard and seen.

"We shall leave this place and not return until the leaves fall," the chief said solemnly. "We must obey the good spirit."

That day the Indians packed all their clothes and food and weapons and left the site. The little Indian babies rode on the backs of their mothers, and the dogs came, too, running alongside the band.

All summer, the Indians stayed away.

When they returned in the fall, they saw great fields of tall green stalks, with golden ears all wrapped in green husks and soft brown silk.

They called it the corn.

The Indians gathered it carefully. They remembered what the good spirit had told the young brave.

Ever since that day, the Indian has used corn, and when the white man came, it was one of the many gifts which he received from our people.

The Corn-Husk Doll

Several days after Nokomis had told the story of the corn, Bedabin remembered the corn husks and cobs in the old box in the storehouse.

She ran swiftly to the house of Nokomis. Her grandmother was sitting on the ground outside, in the warm sun.

"Nokomis, what are you going to do with the cobs and the husks that you took off the corn the other day?" Bedabin asked.

"Some of the husks will be woven into mats. From the cobs we will make mattress fillings to lie on at night."

"And what else will you do with them?" Bedabin pressed.

"Sometimes we make dolls for little girls, if they are good," Nokomis said with a smile on her old face.

"Oh, do make one for me," Bedabin asked. "And let me watch you while you make it."

Nokomis nodded and smiled.

"Very well, bring me a cob and a few husks," she said to her grand-daughter.

Bedabin ran very quickly to the storehouse, lifted the lid of the big box, and took out the longest, fattest cob, and some husks, too.

"This is a good cob," said Nokomis. "You have chosen well."

Bedabin flushed with pleasure. Her grandmother did not praise her very often.

The corn-husk doll.

Nokomis picked up the cob in her strong brown hands and smoothed the husks down around it.

Then she sent Bedabin into the house to fetch her bone needle and her thread.

With the sinew thread, Nokomis began to shape the doll. First she tied a thread around where the neck should be. Then a thread for the waist, and one for each of the arms.

Bedabin grew very excited to see her doll take shape.

Nokomis pulled the thread tightly, and tied it in good strong knots.

"Now we must make some clothes for your doll," said Nokomis.

"But what will we use for them?" asked Bedabin, in a disappointed tone of voice. All she could see were corn husks, and they wouldn't make very beautiful clothes.

"If you look in my birch basket, you will find a small piece of buckskin. We can use that for a dress," said Nokomis.

"That would be perfect," said Bedabin happily. "She will look just like me, because I have a coat of buckskin. It will keep her very warm in winter, too."

Nokomis worked quickly. In and out of the buckskin went the bone needle, and soon she had made a little dress that fitted quite neatly.

"Now your doll needs hair," said Nokomis. "I will use some of the ones from the rabbit your father killed on the last hunt."

"Give her very long hair," insisted Bedabin. "That is most beautiful."

Nokomis gave the doll long hair, and bound it with thread on the top of her head.

"The doll must have some jewellery," said Nokomis. "Gather some tiny seeds, and we will use them to make necklaces and bracelets for around her neck and arms."

"May I use corn kernels?" asked Bedabin.

"We must save those for eating," Nokomis replied. "Remember

what the corn spirit said? Besides, they would be too large for a small doll. Gather the seeds that have fallen from the trees."

So Bedabin crawled on her hands and knees around the base of the old tree near Nokomis's house, and she came back with a whole handful of seeds.

She and her grandmother strung them on very fine strands of sinew, to make long necklaces and short necklaces and three small bracelets.

"Now all we need is a face," Bedabin said, feeling quite pleased that her doll was nearly complete.

"A face? Oh no," said Nokomis, looking very serious. "Our people never make faces on their dolls."

Bedabin was first very surprised, then disappointed. She had wanted so much for her doll to have beautiful, big, dark eyes, and a smiling mouth.

Then she thought carefully about all the dolls that the other girls in the band owned. None of them had faces either. She had never really noticed before.

"But why not have faces?" Bedabin asked earnestly.

"You are a big girl, Bedabin, and you will take care of your doll. But often the little girls like to throw their dolls around. Your little sister will probably do the same with yours. It would hurt much to be tossed about like that.

"Our people believe that anything with a face has a soul, and that anything with a soul can feel pain. So when we make corn-husk dolls, we never make a face. That way the doll will feel no pain when she is thrown around and played with."

Bedabin thought for a few moments. Then she smiled.

"I understand now," she said. "And I like my doll just the way she is."

The Little People

Winter had come to the encampment. It covered the land with a great white blanket, and small ponds of water were frozen over. Sometimes the men went out to hunt in the forest, and sometimes they remained inside the houses, smoking and talking. The women were busy sewing animal skins into warm clothes and blankets for their families. The older children helped their parents, but the younger ones played outdoors in the snow.

Tawa and Bedabin liked to slide on the smooth ice of the stream, and they spent much time outdoors before and after school. But during the long winter evenings, they loved to draw close to Nokomis and listen to tales of her life before the coming of the settlers.

They also told her much about the ways of the white man which they were learning in school. Nokomis found them hard to understand. She had never gone to school. She had lived only by the laws set down by the band leader, and by the laws of nature.

She tried to explain that with the coming of the settlers, the needs of her people had changed. Some of the men worked in the mines and the lumber camps of the white man. On some reserves there were not many animals left to hunt. Her people bought food from the general store instead. Some of the women bought clothes there, too, and no longer made and wore garments of animal skin. Many of the children who now went to school no longer learned from their parents the ancient crafts of their people. Some people had even given up the ancient remedies for sickness, and went to the white man's hospitals and doctors instead.

Nokomis felt it was important to tell the children of the old beliefs, so they would not forget.

"We bury our dead in the ground, and give them enough food and tobacco to last for four days, for it takes that long for them to arrive in the Happy Hunting Ground, the land of the souls in the south. There all the souls dwell in happiness, hunting and dancing and feasting, as on earth. All are dressed in their most beautiful clothing, for that is what we put on them when they die."

"And a chief looks most splendid of all," added Tawa.

"Yes, indeed," said Nokomis. "A chief is given most honour of all in the Happy Hunting Ground. When he dies, we place his body on a high scaffold, to make sure that he is given all the acclaim in the afterlife that he received in this life."

"Does everyone go to the Happy Hunting Ground when they die?" asked Bedabin.

"Oh no," answered Nokomis. "The Little People wander the earth. They remain near their graves, or in the encampments of their people."

"How do they live?" asked Tawa.

"Do you not remember the Festival of the Dead, in the fall of each year?" replied Nokomis. "At that time the living relatives gather and burn a little food for those who have not been fortunate enough to go to the Happy Hunting Ground."

"And everyone feasts and dances until morning," Bedabin added.

"Yes," Nokomis agreed. "The Little People depend on their living relatives to remember."

Nokomis was old now. She often wondered if she would be worthy of the Happy Hunting Ground. Perhaps she would become one of the Little People, instead, because she had accepted some of the ways of the white man.

She hoped that Bedabin and Tawa would not forget to burn food for her.

She told the grandchildren of the days of her grandparents, and how they had explained to her the ways of the Great Spirit.

The Great Manitou, they said, had created the earth and all creatures on it. He had looked after every living thing, punishing them only when they proved unworthy of his gifts. People then had not worried the way they did today. They had trusted more in the Good Spirit.

Her people in those days were not selfish, but shared everything together. Nowadays they were not as willing to give to their neighbours.

What made them think they would ever again be lucky in a hunt, when they hoarded everything for themselves?

The Feast of the Dead

Nokomis's tales of the Little People and the Great Manitou had helped Bedabin and Tawa understand why their parents and their grandmother were so busy and so painstaking with preparations for the Festival of the Dead.

There was much to be done. Nokomis wanted everything to be just right. The great feast was most important, for it was to be given for all of her relatives who had not been worthy to enter the Happy Hunting Ground.

Nokomis had to be sure that nothing was used that had been brought by the white man. Her relatives had never eaten the flesh of domesticated animals such as cows and pigs. She would never think of serving such food.

Muskrat and beaver, deer and moose, and rabbit and partridge would supply the main course of the meal. There would be corn bread, too, made from the lovely white lard of the porcupine. Blueberries and cranberries and many other kinds of wild fruit would also be served.

There would be maple sugar, glazed squash and pumpkin, and wild honey from the hollow of a tree. Beans of all kinds would be boiled and baked for the feast.

Everything had to be made as well as it possibly could be, for Nokomis did not want to do anything to cause the anger of her relatives who had become Little People. These were most

At the Feast of the Dead, food is offered to the Little People, seen at left.

important beings. They would guide you to the Happy Hunting Ground, when it became time for you to make that long journey. If you fell out of favour with them, who would be there to show you the way? Worse still, if they were angry with you, they might lead you on a wild goose chase just to get even.

The day of the feast was cold and cloudy, and snow was falling. Bedabin and Tawa raced home from school, because already friends and relatives would be arriving. Nokomis had set out welcoming bowls of hard maple-sugar candy, fruit juice, and many kinds of fruit glazed with honey.

At nightfall every relative had arrived. No one would have thought of staying away, no matter what the weather.

When old and young were seated at the tables, Tawa's father rose to give a long prayer. He spoke in the Ojibwa language, which none of the children understood, for they spoke English at home and at school.

Nokomis explained to her grandchildren that the Ojibwa words were first of all a welcome to the Little People. They were also a greeting to all the relatives gathered around the table to honour the Little People.

Nokomis then took a plate from the head of the table. On it she placed a little of every kind of food. It was a very colourful plate – yellow and green and orange and white.

Then she walked solemnly to the fireplace, and cast the food into the fire.

Everyone sat with bowed head until each morsel had been consumed in the flames.

"Why did you do that?" asked Tawa, in a whisper, after all had raised their heads.

Nokomis explained that the Little People were spirits, and therefore invisible. So of course the food that they ate had to be invisible, too – it had to be turned into smoke.

Now that the ceremony was over, all the guests ate to their heart's content. It wasn't often that one had such a delicious meal.

And it was great fun to see all the relatives together. These occasions were very rare and much to be treasured.

Spring in the Forest

One fine Saturday morning in early spring, Bedabin and Tawa bounded into Nokomis's room with light steps. Spring had really come at last.

"Come on, Nokomis," said Tawa, gently nudging the shoulder of his grandmother to waken her. "The snow is all gone, and Bedabin and you and I are all going to take a walk down through the forest to the lake."

"It is a beautiful morning," said Bedabin with joy. "The sky is very blue, and the sun is warm. You won't feel the cold at all. Do come with us," she urged.

Tears of joy sprang into Nokomis's old eyes to think that once more she could walk through the forest she loved so well.

Quickly she rose from her bed by the fire. She pulled on her leggings of moose skin, and tied them just below the knee. Then she put on her moccasins, her long sleeves, and her mittens, all made of moose skin. She wasn't going to wear her cap today, because it was spring, and she wanted to feel the cool, fresh air about her head. Soon she would have to wear only her skirt and blouse and moccasins. Then she would know for sure that summer had come. But she was an old woman, and it was better to dress warmly now, so as not to catch cold.

Soon she was ready, and set off down the path to the lake with Bedabin and Tawa. The children would dash on ahead to explore, and then would run back to rejoin their grandmother.

Nokomis did not mind. She walked along at her own pace, and felt very happy. The air was sweet to breathe, and filled with the songs of her friends, the birds. They were all talking at once. The ones that had flown south for the winter had now returned, and they were all building their nests, and flying high overhead in graceful curves.

Bedabin came running down the path to her grandmother.

"Tawa's exploring the old sugar camp," she said, nearly out of breath. "He said the whole band will go there soon to gather the sap from the maple trees."

"That's right," answered Nokomis with a smile. "You remember how we go there every spring when the sap is running. It is very important to gather as much as we can to keep for the winter when we will have less to eat."

"Soon our people will be going again," she said. "Then you will be able to watch them harden the sap."

"It tastes so good," said Bedabin. "Everyone eats so much."

"It's the most delicious food of all," said Tawa, joining his sister and grandmother. "I can hardly wait for the time to come."

"It will soon be here," Nokomis assured him. "Spring has surely come. Do you see that small, pink flower?"

"Where?" said Tawa.

"I see it," said Bedabin. "It has a lovely smell."

"That's called Trailing Arbutus," said Nokomis. "When you see it, you know for sure that spring has come. There is a story about that."

"Do tell us," asked Bedabin.

She moved closer to her grandmother, to be certain to hear every word.

A long time ago there lived a very old chief who knew that his time to travel to the Happy Hunting Ground was not far off.

He had been a very wise and much-loved chief, and didn't want to leave his people without something that would remind them of

The spirit of the Trailing Arbutus.

him, and of all the things he had taught them.

One night, in his sleep, the good spirit came to him in the form of a beautiful maiden.

"Who are you?" asked the old chief.

"I am Hope," answered the maiden. "Without me, your people would grow discontented during the long, cold winters. I am here to help you."

"What can I leave to my people?" asked the old chief.

"I will offer myself," the maiden replied, "as a sacrifice to spring. When your people see me growing in the form of a trailing plant with pink flowers, they will know that the long winter is past, and that the lovely spring is at hand."

"Now you know what the Trailing Arbutus means," Nokomis concluded. "Spring is here for sure."

The First Water Lily

Once upon a time there was a large band of Indians who spent their summers beside a lake, close to a big mountain.

The lake gave them cool, sweet water to drink, and for cooking. It also gave them fish to eat.

In the forest on the mountain lived many small animals. The Indian men would go with their bows and arrows and knives to hunt them. They would never kill any more animals than necessary to provide food for all the people in the band.

One morning, one of the braves of the band decided to visit one of his friends, the Owl. Everyone knows that the owl sleeps in the day and stays awake at night. So the young Indian man had to visit his friend when it was still dark.

He left his wigwam very early in the morning and looked up at the sky to see if the sun had started to take off his night cloak. But everything was still very black.

Suddenly the young man saw a beautiful star hanging over the camp. It was very big, and very, very bright. The brave had never seen such a lovely star in his whole life.

He was quite frightened, for perhaps it was a sign that something dreadful was going to occur.

The young brave rushed around to all the wigwams of the chiefs of the band, and woke them all up.

"Come and see a beautiful, big star!" he exclaimed. "What do you think it means?"

The wise old chiefs all came out of their wigwams, sat in a circle looking up at the star. They thought and thought. The star meant something, but what could it mean? Maybe it was there for a good reason? Perhaps it was a kind and beautiful spirit who had come to guard the camp? But maybe it was there for a bad reason? Perhaps some dreadful calamity was coming to the camp?

The chiefs decided to waken the wisest of all the medicine-men. Perhaps he could tell them what the star meant.

But even the medicine-man could not tell them the reason.

The chiefs sat in a circle, looking more and more worried.

"Perhaps," said Chief Rain Cloud, "the star is here to warn us of something dreadful that is about to happen, so we can prepare for it."

"How can we prepare for it if we don't know what it's going to be?" asked Chief Red Sky.

"Maybe the animals are going to war on us for eating some of their friends," suggested Chief Hungry Eyes.

But the wisest of all, Chief Friend of Owl, said, "Let's go and ask our friend, the Owl, what we should do."

Everyone agreed and they all went together to see the owl. It was still dark, and Owl had not yet gone to sleep.

"Wise owl," said Chief Friend of Owl, "there is a great star hovering over our encampment! What does it mean? What should we do about it?"

"Go and ask her," said wise Owl bluntly.

The chiefs chose Red Sky to climb the mountain to speak with star and find out what she wanted.

Red Sky climbed as high as he possibly could, so that he would not have to shout to the star. Finally he reached the top of the mountain and spoke to the star.

"Great star, do not be angry with me for asking many questions, but we are all very worried. You are a very beautiful

The Water Lily

star, but we do not understand why you are hanging over our camp. Would you kindly tell me why you do this?"

The lovely star shone even more brightly. She smiled on Red Sky, and answered, "For many days I have been watching your people. They are very happy, especially the children playing by the lake, and the babies in their cradles of birch bark on their mothers' backs. If I am welcome, I would like very much to come and live amongst your people."

Chief Red Sky smiled with joy. He was so happy with the news he was to bring to his people that he ran down the mountain as fast as he could go.

When he neared the camp, he shouted with a loud voice, "Come out, come out. I have great news for all to hear."

When all of the band, fathers and mothers and children, the very old and the very young, and all the dogs, had gathered outside their wigwams, Red Sky spoke.

The great star finds us a happy people. She would like to come and live amongst us. That is why she has been hanging over our camp."

Everyone rejoiced.

The chiefs held a council. It was wonderful, they all felt, to have such a great star for a friend. No doubt the heavens would smile on them if this beautiful star were living amongst them.

They decided that Chief Fire Cloud should officially welcome her to their band. He must also tell her that she should feel free to live wherever she chose. All of the band would be pleased with whatever she decided.

Chief Fire Cloud climbed the mountain right to the top, and delivered the message of the chiefs. The star shone brightly. She was happy to be invited to live with these people.

Now she had to decide where to dwell.

First she tried the mountain top. But she soon decided that it was too far away from the people.

Then she tried the top of the highest tree in the forest. But the foliage was so thick that she couldn't see the people.

Poor star. She didn't know what to do. She decided to return to the sky and think the problem over.

She thought and thought, and suddenly she had the best idea. On the lake, beside the camp – that would be the perfect spot. There she would be able to see the women with the papooses on their backs, and the children at play, and the braves singing as they built their birch-bark canoes.

That night she floated gently down and settled on the water.

The next morning when the Indians came down to the water's edge, there she was in all her splendour – the first Water Lily.

The Legend of the Birch Tree

A very long time ago, long before there were people living in this beautiful land, the trees could talk with one another. When they rustled, that was quiet talk. But when they bent swiftly to and fro in a fierce wind, their words were full of courage or of fear.

There were many different kinds of trees in the forest.

The lovely Maple tree had sweet sap to give to the birds when they grew thirsty. Many birds made nests in her limbs. There the round nests of the robin, filled with small, pale blue eggs, as blue as the sky on a fair day. Maple kept them safe from wind and rain. She was a very kind tree, always ready to give something that was needed. She was highly respected by the other trees.

Then there was the tall Elm who would stretch her limbs very high. How she loved the sun. She was a graceful tree, and spread her arms out evenly all around. The orioles made their long, swinging nests in her boughs. They felt safe there, so far above the ground.

Also in the forest grew the beautiful Cedar. The birds flocked to her boughs in the winter. She would fold her thick arms around them on the coldest nights, and keep them snug and warm. She was so sweet and fresh they would have stayed there willingly for a long time.

The fair Birch tree also grew here. She was slender and graceful, with pure white skin that was very soft. Her arms were fair and supple, and she swayed gently with every breeze. In the spring her leaves were pale green, and so fine that the sun shone right through them. When our people came to this land they used the fair birch to make their canoes and their wigwams and even the vessels in which they cooked their food.

But poor Birch! Although she was fair, she was also proud, and she was soon to learn her lesson.

The stately evergreen Pine was king of the forest. To him every tree would bow her head. For did he not look like a king? He was the tallest of all, and so very straight, and dressed in a magnificent blue-green robe.

One fine summer day, the forest was abloom with all kinds and colours of flowers, and a soft carpet of moss spread over the forest floor. Small birds and large birds, and red and yellow and blue birds were singing gaily. The trees were rustling swiftly and lightly, for they were laughing and chatting.

Maple suddenly noticed that Birch was not joining in the fun.

"Are you ill, dear Birch?" asked the kindly Maple.

"Not at all," answered Birch pertly, tossing her fair limbs. "I never felt better in my life. But why should anyone as fair as myself bother with the rest of you? You are all so plain."

Maple tree was sad, for she knew that Pine would be very angry if he heard. He was a good king, and always made the other trees behave themselves. He set a good example, too.

"Hush, Birch," said the other trees. "Do you want Pine to hear you?"

The trees were used to standing up for one another. They tried to help each other, like brothers and sisters.

But Birch would have nothing to do with anyone. She tossed her limbs with even more disdain, and swayed to and fro stubbornly.

"Who cares about Pine?" she said. "I am fairer than any tree in the forest, and I will no longer bow down to Pine."

Pine, who had been taking a nap, awoke with a start when he

Pine Tree whips the proud Birch with his branches.

heard his name mentioned. He shook his sharp needles to arrange them in place, and he stood up even straighter than before, stretching.

"Tell me, Birch, what was that you were just saying?"

Poor Birch. Pine could not have been sleeping very soundly. All the trees trembled, for they knew that their king could become very angry.

But Birch had no fear. She calmly swept her gracious limbs from side to side, and answered haughtily.

"I am no longer going to bow down to you, Pine. I am the most beautiful tree in the whole forest, more lovely than all the other trees, lovelier even than you. All the trees should bow down to me."

Pine was very angry, and his limbs began to shake. The heavy blue boughs swayed from side to side, and all the other trees trembled in perfect silence.

"Birch," he roared, "you have become too vain. I shall have to teach you a lesson that you will always remember."

With that, he bent way over towards Birch, and switched her fair skin very hard with his sharp needles.

"May all who see you learn from your example," he said more quietly.

If you look closely today at the fair white bark of the Birch, you will find small, thin, brown scars – the price she paid for vanity so long ago.

The First Lady's Slipper

One day, Bedabin, running ahead of Tawa and her grandmother, suddenly cried out, "Oh look, Nokomis, look at this lovely moccasin."

Old Nokomis was much slower than the children, but finally she reached the spot in the trail where Bedabin was bending over the small flower. It was a beautiful yellow colour, with waxy petals.

"It looks just like my moccasin," said Bedabin excitedly.

"Some people call it a Lady's Slipper," said Nokomis wisely. "It really should be called a Moccasin Flower, because that's how it first came to be."

"Many years ago no one lived in this forest but our forefathers," Nokomis said solemnly. "That was long before the white man came."

"Did your grandmother live here?" interrupted Bedabin.

"Yes, and her grandmother before her," replied Nokomis.

"And your grandfather?" asked Tawa.

"He, too," said Nokomis.

"Oh," said the children together, wide-eyed. That seemed almost longer than they could imagine.

For many years, this forest was the summer home of our people. They spent the warm summer months here, beside the lake where it was cool. There were many fish in the lake. The forest beside the lake provided shade from the summer heat, and shelter from the sudden summer rain storms.

But as soon as the leaves began to fall from the trees, their wise chief knew that it was time for them to start preparing for the move to the winter camp. There they would be warm and sheltered during the long months of heavy snow. And there in the thick forest would be moose in abundance, to provide them with food during the winter.

Travelling to the winter camp took many days. The arrival of the first frost warned the people to prepare for the journey. The young braves prepared the canoes, and gathered together all their hunting equipment, their bows and arrows and spears. The women of the band packed the clothes and blankets made of animal hides. They also gathered together all the precious food – berries, herbs, maize and wild rice – they had dried and prepared during the summer months, for the long winter months ahead.

Finally all was ready, and a day was set for departure.

The wise chief would lead the way. He knew best which paths to follow so that the women with little papooses on their backs, and the small children clinging to their mother's skirts would find the easiest walking. He knew where to find the clearest springs, to refresh his people as they travelled. He also knew how long the mothers and little children could travel before they grew too tired.

Before dusk, the wise chief would call a halt.

The band would unpack just what they needed for that evening. The women would go into the woods to gather some long poles for the wigwams. The men would help them stick these in the ground in a round circle, and lash them together at the top. Over the poles, bark would be placed to keep out the cold.

Then some of the women would build a fire in the centre of the wigwam, to prepare the evening meal.

Other women would prepare the beds for the evening. Around the fire they would place fir boughs. On top of these they would place animal hides, and here they would sleep, with more animal skins covering them.

While the men and women were working, the children would play at hide-and-seek and games of make believe.

One time when the children were playing, one small maiden wandered away from the group. She wasn't even missed until everyone had gathered for the evening meal.

They ate very quickly, and started looking for her. They looked long into the night, calling with loud voices, and waving their torches about, but no little girl answered. She was not to be found.

Early the next morning, the wise chief called the people together. He told them that they would have all that day to look for the little girl. But the following day even if the little girl had not been found, they would have to resume their journey to the winter camp.

Everyone looked very hard, even the very old and the very young. All were worried. They had all liked the little girl. She was pretty, and very good. She must be very hungry.

When the sun was high in the sky, one of the braves found one small moccasin. But no little girl. Many looked near the place where the small leather shoe had been found, and they called and called. But no one answered.

The mother and father were heart-broken. They knew their people would have to move on the next day to the winter camp. The cold weather was approaching soon.

The next morning they woke up early. Together they made a small hole in the ground. In it they placed the moccasin, and covered it with earth. Over it, they built a marker.

The women gathered together the food, and the men their hunting equipment, their canoes, and the rolls of birch bark from the wigwams. They made their way together to the winter camp.

The snow fell deep upon the ground, and lasted for many months. Often through the long cold months, the parents of the little girl thought about her. When she was cooking food over the

The little girl has reached the Happy Hunting Ground, shown by the red lines. The birds and circles represent peace and happiness.

fire in the wigwam, the mother thought of her. When he was hunting moose in the dark forest, the father thought of her.

Finally spring came. The snow melted all away. The buds on the trees appeared, and burst into bright green leaves. The birds sang joyfully. It was time for the band to return to their summer camp.

As they journeyed back through the forest, the parents of the little girl kept watch for the place where they had buried the tiny moccasin. Suddenly, they came upon it.

There in the very spot where the marker had been grew a beautiful little yellow flower, shaped just like the small moccasin. Then they were very happy, for they knew that this was the Great Manitou's way of telling them that their little girl had reached the Happy Hunting Ground.

The Legend of the Oriole

Nokomis loved the warm summer days. She was an old woman, and the cold made her ache all over.

But now it was summer, and the sky was very blue. The sun was bright, and the little ripples on the lake sparkled like small drops of dew. The birds of the forest were singing all at once, and the leaves of the trees were rustling in the wind.

Nokomis was going for a walk with her grandchildren. Today they were going to the big hill, about a mile away from camp. Bedabin wanted to look for flowers, and Tawa wanted to find lots of berries. Both of them wanted to watch the birds.

Tawa and Bedabin especially wished to watch the oriole. They had spent many hours lying flat on the ground beneath an elm tree, as still as possible, to see these beautiful birds build their long nests and feed their young. The male bird was especially beautiful, for he had a bright orange breast and a deep black back.

When the orioles built their nests they worked very carefully, weaving fine twigs and grass in and out to make a strong home in which to raise their young.

Some oriole nests lasted for two or three years, they were so strong. But the birds only used them once. They would build their nests in a different place each year.

Bedabin and Tawa had tried very hard to look inside the nests, but they had never succeeded. It was easy to climb the big elm,

The grateful Oriole sings to greet the Sun.

even up to the highest limb. But the orioles always built their nests away out on the very end of the branch, and not even Tawa dared climb out there. What if the limb should break? Oh, poor Tawa!

Today they would not try to climb the elm. Instead, they would lie very quietly on the ground to watch the orioles feed their young.

Nokomis sat down near them in the shade of an old tree. She leaned against the trunk, and shut her eyes for a short nap.

Bedabin and Tawa lay on their stomachs on the soft green moss to watch the birds in the big elm.

They lay very still for a long, long time.

After a while, Nokomis stirred and rubbed her eyes.

"Do you know why the oriole is such a beautiful bird?" she asked with a smile.

"Weren't they always this lovely?" Tawa wanted to know.

"Oh, no," said Nokomis.

At one time the oriole was a plain, grey, little bird. His coat of grey was very dull. But he had a beautiful voice, and every morning he sang a song to greet the sun as he came up over the edge of the forest.

All the other birds ignored the plain little oriole. The poor bird felt quite lonely. But he kept on singing to the Sun each day.

Sun loved the oriole very much for the beautiful melody with which he was greeted each morning. It made Sun feel very joyous, and he shone even more brightly than usual.

One morning, after oriole had sung his song, Sun said to him, "I wish to do something for you, because you have been so friendly. I will grant you one wish. Think hard before you make it, because there can be only one."

"I wish to be beautiful," oriole said at once. All his life he had wanted this, and he had known right away what to say.

Sun said no more, but went on his way further up the sky.

Later in the day, when Sun was almost directly overhead, the oriole flew over a pond. He looked into the still water, and saw a beautiful orange and black bird.

How surprised he was, and how full of joy. He could hardly stop singing.

"Now all the other birds will play with me, and I won't be lonely any more," he sang joyfully.

The next morning, because he was so grateful, he sang all the harder to greet the Sun.

Sun was pleased at the small bird's joy, and happy that oriole had remembered to say thank you. He smiled warmly, and said, "You are now beautiful on the outside, but your beautiful song and your beautiful soul give me even more pleasure. You will always remain lovely, as long as you continue to sing your song to the world.

"I will teach you how to build your nests in safe places out on the highest limbs, and no one will ever learn the secret of how you weave them there. In this way I will know that there will always be orioles to greet the sunrise."

Nokomis's Last Sunset

Many years passed and Bedabin and Tawa grew up. Both married and had children of their own. They no longer lived in their childhood home, but often they would come back to visit the places they had known long ago with Nokomis, before she had taken that journey to the Happy Hunting Ground of her fathers.

Her wise teaching had helped Bedabin and Tawa many times throughout their lives, and their little children begged to hear the stories that Nokomis had long ago loved to tell.

One evening, while Bedabin was visiting the place of her birth, she stood at the edge of the lake near Nokomis's old home. Evening was drawing near, and Bedabin gazed out over the water at the setting sun, hanging low in the sky like a great ball of fire.

"Bedabin, Bedabin," someone called softly.

She turned to see Tawa standing near.

Bedabin held out her hand to him. Together they watched the big ball of fire sink slowly into the water. It seemed almost as if the water were putting out the sun.

But even after the sun had completely disappeared, where water and sky met there remained a red glow, like tongues of flame shooting up into the sky and reflecting on the water.

Many times before they had stood with Nokomis, watching just such a sunset.

"It seems she is here right now," said Tawa.

"I was thinking that, too," replied Bedabin.

"We will remember, Nokomis," promised Tawa.

"To put out food for the Little People. . .

"And to watch for the trailing arbutus in the spring. . .

"And the small yellow moccasin flower. . .

"And the star that became a water lily. . .

"And the birch tree that was whipped. . .

"And the oriole whose song was rewarded. . .

"And the gift of corn. . .

"And the red and white Trilliums. . .

"And how the Indian Paint Brush came to be. . .

"And so many other stories. . .

"And we will tell our children," said Bedabin, "and they will tell theirs, who will tell theirs."

"Your stories will never be forgotten," said Tawa.